P9-CJL-853

Dear Parents:

Congratulations! Your child is taking the first steps on an exciting journey. The destination? Independent reading!

STEP INTO READING® will help your child get there. The program offers five steps to reading success. Each step includes fun stories and colorful art or photographs. In addition to original fiction and books with favorite characters, there are Step into Reading Non-Fiction Readers, Phonics Readers and Boxed Sets, Sticker Readers, and Comic Readers—a complete literacy program with something to interest every child.

Learning to Read, Step by Step!

Ready to Read   Preschool–Kindergarten
• big type and easy words • rhyme and rhythm • picture clues
For children who know the alphabet and are eager to begin reading.

Reading with Help   Preschool–Grade 1
• basic vocabulary • short sentences • simple stories
For children who recognize familiar words and sound out new words with help.

Reading on Your Own   Grades 1–3
• engaging characters • easy-to-follow plots • popular topics
For children who are ready to read on their own.

Reading Paragraphs   Grades 2–3
• challenging vocabulary • short paragraphs • exciting stories
For newly independent readers who read simple sentences with confidence.

Ready for Chapters   Grades 2–4
• chapters • longer paragraphs • full-color art
For children who want to take the plunge into chapter books but still like colorful pictures.

STEP INTO READING® is designed to give every child a successful reading experience. The grade levels are only guides; children will progress through the steps at their own speed, developing confidence in their reading.

Remember, a lifetime love of reading starts with a single step!

Visit us on the Web!
StepIntoReading.com
randomhousekids.com

Educators and librarians, for a variety of teaching tools, visit us at RHTeachersLibrarians.com

ISBN 978-0-553-50853-6 (trade) — ISBN 978-0-553-50855-0 (lib. bdg.)

Printed in the United States of America   *5543 9201*   *0/15*

10 9 8 7 6 5 4 3 2 1

nickelodeon

PIT CREW PUPS

PAW PATROL

By Kristen Depken

Based on the teleplay "Pups Pit Crew"
by Franklin Young

Illustrated by MJ Illustrations

Random House 🏠 New York

Alex is a friend
of the PAW Patrol.
He builds
a Super Trike.

He wants
to go super fast!
He shows
his grandpa.

Alex puts on
his helmet.

Alex pedals.

The trike falls apart!

The parts go

everywhere!

Who can help?

The PAW Patrol!

Alex's grandpa

calls Ryder.

The pups are ready
to help.
Here they come!

Chase directs traffic.
Ryder and Alex pick up
the trike parts.

Rocky brings the parts
to the garage.
He and Ryder
put the trike
back together.

Alex's Super Trike
is even better
than before.

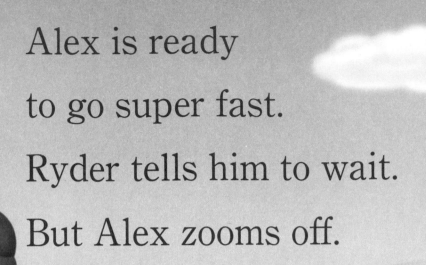

Alex is ready

to go super fast.

Ryder tells him to wait.

But Alex zooms off.

Alex speeds
down a hill.
He goes too fast.
He cannot stop!

The pups chase
after him.
He races toward
the busy street!

Chase stops
the traffic
just in time.

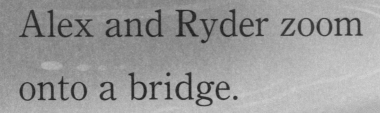

Alex and Ryder zoom
onto a bridge.

Ryder calls Skye.
She flies her helicopter
over the bridge.
She spots Alex and
hooks on to his trike.

The trike stops!

Alex is safe.

He cheers and waves

to Skye.

Alex thanks Ryder
and the pups.
Next time,
he will slow down.

Ryder and the pups
take Alex
to get lemonade.

The pups show Alex
how to ride safely.

Ryder gives Alex
a prize for
safe driving.
Hooray for Alex!